Simone™

Joins the
SOCCER TEAM

By Dr. Kelsi Bracmort • Illustrated by Takeia Marie

Publisher's Cataloging-in-Publication Data

Names: Bracmort, Kelsi, author. | Marie, Takeia, illustrator.
Title: Simone joins the soccer team / by Dr. Kelsi Bracmort; illustrated by Takeia Marie.
Description: Washington, D.C.: Mayhew Pursuits LLC, 2021. | Summary: Simone, a vibrant African-American girl from Washington, DC, seeks advice from family and friends as she contemplates trying out for her school's soccer team.
Identifiers: LCCN: 2020947518| ISBN: 978-0-9995685-6-9 (Hardcover) | 978-0-9995685-7-6 (paperback) | 978-0-9995685-8-3 (ebook)
Subjects: LCSH Soccer--Fiction. | Family--Juvenile fiction. | African Americans--Juvenile fiction. | Self-acceptance--Juvenile fiction. | Self-confidence--Juvenile fiction. | Washington (D.C.)--Juvenile fiction. | BISAC JUVENILE FICTION / People & Places / United States / African American | JUVENILE FICTION / Sports & Recreation / Soccer | JUVENILE FICTION / Girls & Women | JUVENILE FICTION / Lifestyles / City & Town Life
Classification: LCC PZ7.1 B7155 Sim 2021 | DDC [E]--dc23

The text for this book is set in Poppins.
The illustrations for this book were rendered digitally.

For my sister, Kristen. I love you.
—K.B.

It's Monday afternoon, and Simone and her cousin Shiloh
hold hands as they climb a steep hill, taking the brick steps
two at a time. They're headed to the Frederick Douglass home.
It's their favorite after-school hangout where they can talk
without a lot of other kids around.

When they get to the front porch, Simone starts to bop side to side as she looks out across the Anacostia streets. She suddenly twirls and blurts out, "I think I want to join the soccer team." She sees Shiloh furrow her eyebrows. "Soccer tryouts are this week. Kicking that ball looks fun!"

Without missing a beat, Shiloh says, "So . . . do it."
She slings her sky-blue braids over her left shoulder as she
sits down on a step. "But . . . you know the soccer team
practices like three times a week and you have to go to
every game. That's a lot. Are you sure?"

Simone dribbles an imaginary soccer ball. "Yeah, I know. I'm going to ask my parents about it."

Shiloh stands up. "Simone," she says, mimicking her Aunt's sincere voice, "Is this something you truly want to do? Will you be able to play soccer and maintain your grades?"

Simone giggles. "Maybe I'll talk to Daddy about it first."

After a few more minutes of talking on the porch, they start the short walk to Shiloh's house a few blocks away. They each eat a green apple-flavored rock candy stick. They speak to Ms. Mae as she crochets a baby blanket while sitting in a rocking chair on her front porch. They pet her son's dog Ginger and she licks their fingers. When they turn the corner, Simone's father is leaning on his car waiting to take her home.

"Daddy!" Simone shouts as she runs to hug him.

"Hey Unc," Shiloh says giving him a high five.

With Simone's arms wrapped around his waist, he asks, "Did you have a good day at school?"

"Yep," they reply in unison.

"Cool. Shiloh, tell your mother we'll see her later. Simone, let's roll."

As they drive home, Simone's father glances in the rearview mirror at her. "Honey, what's new today?"

"Daddy, I . . . I think I want to play soccer. Tryouts are later this week," Simone says as she stares out the window.

Her father turns down the volume on the car radio. "Do you think or do you know?"

Simone looks at her father and leans forward. "I've never played a team sport before. But I think I'll like playing soccer."

"Soccer is a wonderful sport. You'll get to learn from others and cooperate with your teammates, and you'll have to respect the decision of the referees. Well, think about it and let me and Mommy know what you decide. We support whatever decision you make," her father says.

"Thanks, Daddy."

After an early dinner, Simone's mother drops her and her brother Scott off at church for youth choir practice. As Scott and the other young musicians set up their equipment, Simone takes a seat in the third pew.

DeAndre, her classmate who also lives in her neighborhood, joins her in the pew. "What's wrong, Simone? Why are you sitting here instead of in the choir section?"

"I'm thinking. I want to play soccer, but I don't know if I'll be good at it," she says.

DeAndre slouches down in the pew. "Nah, you wouldn't be any good at that. That's not your thing," he says as he scrunches up his face like it's a ridiculous thought.

Simone squints at him. "Why do you say that?"

"'Cause I've never seen you play anything," he replies as he kicks the back of the pew in front of them.

"Hey!" the youth choir director, Ms. Eliza, calls out to them sharply. "DeAndre, Simone, it's time to practice. Up here . . . now."

Simone darts past DeAndre and rushes up front to join the others. She loves to sing, but right now, all she can think about is if she should try out for the soccer team. She can't wait to get home so she can think in peace without DeAndre annoying her.

Later that evening in bed, Simone prays and thinks about what she is grateful for. She also replays in her mind what she heard from Shiloh, her father, and DeAndre.

"That's a lot . . . We support you . . . That's not your thing . . . Do you think or do you know . . . "

Simone thinks soccer will be fun. She wants to run, score a goal, and cheer on her teammates. But she also has her doubts. Is she fast enough? What if she misses a goal? What if her teammates don't like her? Maybe she shouldn't give soccer a try.

The next morning Simone gets ready for school. As she brushes her teeth, she decides that she's not going to try out for the soccer team. She's going to play it safe and stick to her normal routine . . . go to school and then go home.

"Nope, not going to do it," she says to herself.

Simone has made her decision, but she's not certain it's the right decision.

After school, Simone walks down the hallway toward the exit. She sees the P.E. teacher Ms. Washington working on a new bulletin board. "Hi, Ms. Washington. What are you putting up?"

Ms. Washington staples a picture to the board. "It's a soccer position chart and pictures of some of the best soccer players in the world."

"Oh." Simone picks up an orange marker. "I thought about trying out for the soccer team tomorrow but decided not to."

"Why not?" Ms. Washington asks.

Simone leans on the wall. "It's not my thing and it would take up a lot of my time."

"Hmmm. That doesn't sound like you, Simone. You're good at managing your time and a quick study. Please reconsider trying out for the team. I think you'd do great," Ms. Washington says while Simone puts the marker back in its box. "And remember, some of these amazing soccer players started out as a little girl just like you."

The next morning soccer is still on Simone's mind when her mother peeks into the bedroom to wake her up for school.

"Good morning, my beautiful Simone," her mother says with a bright smile.

"Good morning, Mommy," Simone says sadly.

Her mother walks in and sits on Simone's bed. "Simone, is everything okay?"

"Mommy, I don't know what to do. I really wanted to try out for the soccer team, but then DeAndre said it wasn't my thing, and Shiloh said it would take up a lot of my time. I decided not to try out. But then Ms. Washington at school said I should reconsider. I don't know. I don't know." Exasperated, Simone lays her head on her mother's shoulder.

"Okay, Simone, calm down. It will be all right, let's talk about it," her mother says.

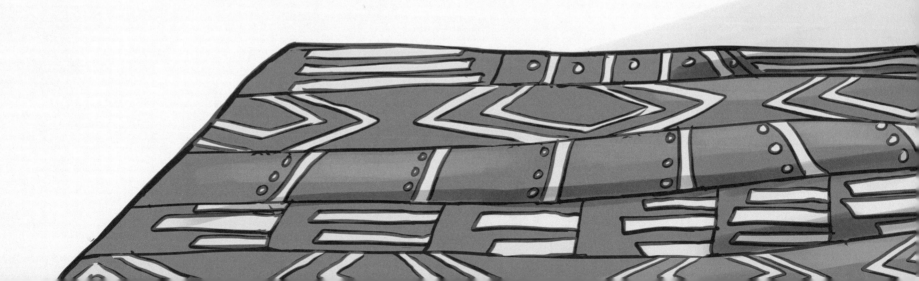

"What do you want to do, Simone?" her mother asks.

Simone thinks for a second, "I want to play soccer."

Her mother nods and asks, "So what's stopping you?"

"Shiloh, DeAndre . . ."

"Wait," her mother interrupts. "Other people, Simone, the answer is other people. You are allowing others to stop you from doing what you want. As long as it doesn't hurt you or anyone else, let those other people live their life and you live yours. Sure, it's wise to get input from people that care about you, but you make decisions for your life based on what you want. What do I always tell you?" her mother asks as she holds Simone's hands. "Here's a hint . . . it involves running."

"Run my own race, don't look to the side, don't look back, look forward to my goal and stay focused," Simone replies.

Her mother smiles. "Simone, do what you want to do for yourself."

Simone, Scott, and their mother are about to walk out the front door to go to school. Simone suddenly runs back to her room. She grabs her hot pink running shoes, her navy-blue gym shorts, and her t-shirt that says "Courage" on the front and throws it all in her metallic purple gym bag, then runs back to the front door. She doesn't know if she will try out for the soccer team after school, but she wants to be prepared if she does.

During lunch, Simone asks for a hall pass. She goes straight to the bulletin board Ms. Washington put up. She slides down the wall across from the board and sits cross-legged on the floor. She looks at the pictures of the soccer players and closes her eyes.

When she's uncertain, "indecisive" Daddy calls it, he tells her to close her eyes and visualize. Simone closes her eyes, and suddenly she's in her navy-blue gym shorts with her hair pulled back. The soccer ball is rolling toward her and she push-passes the ball to a teammate. She runs down the grass field with her team. A teammate passes the ball back to her. Simone kicks the ball with all her strength. It shoots past the goalie. She scores! Her teammates are smiling. This is what she wants.

When she opens her eyes, she can feel the smile across her face. Her mind is made up. She is going to try out for the soccer team!

After school, Simone puts on her gym clothes and goes to the field. Her science class partner Hayley is there, and so is Talia from her reading group. There are also a few other girls she knows in the small group trying out. Her mother and Shiloh are in the stands rooting her on, with other kids' parents and friends.

Ms. Washington patiently explains the drills to them.
The tryout is the first time that several of the girls have played soccer. They dribble the ball, they kick the ball, they practice throwing the ball from inside the penalty box. Simone shouts "Great pass!" to Talia and "Good kick!" to Hayley. Simone is upbeat and she puts forth maximum effort for each drill.

Once tryouts are over, Simone grabs her stuff. Shiloh comes up to her and says, "You did that! You were awesome as goalie! When the ball came toward you, you jumped right out there and grabbed it!"

With a big smile on her face, Simone says, "I felt good out there, Shiloh, like I could do anything!"

Her mother joins them and says, "Great job, Simone!" as she gives her a big hug.

PHWEEEEEEET!!! Ms. Washington blows a whistle and asks the students to settle down.

"Thank you all for showing up. Everyone did a great job today. You showed tremendous effort, and I'm happy to announce that everyone made the team."

Cheers erupt from both the students and the parents.

"One more thing," shouts Ms. Washington as she turns toward Simone. "The team captain will be Simone. You encouraged everyone as we went through the drills. Good job. I'll see you all tomorrow after school for our first practice."

Simone high fives both her mother and Shiloh. She's delighted at having made the team and being selected as team captain. She twirls and twirls and twirls. With the help of her mother and father, Simone listened to her inner voice and did what felt right for her. She can't wait to start soccer practice and lead her team to victory.

About the Author

Dr. Kelsi Bracmort loves living in Washington, D.C. She was inspired to write this book to show the pride, beauty, and diversity she sees in Washington, D.C. every day. It is her desire that this book will be one method to express to the children living in Washington, D.C. that they should listen to their inner voice and go achieve what they want.

About the Illustrator

Takeia Marie is an illustrator from New York, comic book nerd, lover of food, and self-proclaimed hip-hop enthusiast. She enjoys working with businesses and individuals with big ideas, having worked with clients such as The Mill, Goode Stuff Publishing, Action Lab, Brooklyn College Community Partnership, and more. Her work has been published in the Glyph Pioneer Award winning anthology, Artists Against Police Brutality, and has been featured in Black Comix Returns: African-American Comic Art & Culture. She believes that great stories have the power to change people, change minds, and change the world.

CPSIA information can be obtained
at www.ICGtesting.com
Printed in the USA
LVRC101446051021
699594LV00003B/23